The Forever Forest

Kids Save a Tropical Treasure

Kristin Joy Pratt-Serafini
with Rachel Crandell

Dawn Publications

Morpho Butterfly
(Morpho peleides limpida)

Yum, yum, rotting fruit! Unlike most butterflies, which sip nectar from flowers, Blue Morphos love to uncurl their long proboscises into sweet rotting fruit and slurp up the juices through their straw-like tongues. The bright blue that flashes in the sunlight is not really blue. The iridescent color is created in your eye because of the shape and angle of the scales of the butterfly, not from pigment in the scales. Morphos are optical engineers! Their big wings flop slowly and create a "flash defense" by exposing the bright blue from the top of the wings, alternating with drab brown on the underside. They seem to appear and disappear in flashes. They are almost invisible when they land and close their wings.

Heliconia
(Heliconia monteverdensis)

Heliconia's bright red brachts attract hummingbirds to the small yellow blossoms. But it takes a lot of energy for plants to make the color red—botanists say that red is an "expensive" color. So rather than make the red blossom and lose it over and over, Heliconia makes a red bract—a permanent part of the plant.

Peter scampered down the shady trail after the biggest butterfly he had ever seen.
It flapped through a patch of sunlight, showing off its shiny blue wings.

"Look, Mom — a Blue Morpho! I've seen it in books—but it's way bigger than I imagined!" Peter was taking in all the sights, smells and sounds of his first trip to a tropical rainforest.

Peter was excited to spend some of his summer break in Costa Rica with his mom. They had come all the way from Sweden to visit the Children's Eternal Rainforest, or *El Bosque Eterno de los Niños*. Peter just called it "the BEN."

"I think we're almost there," said Anna, jogging to catch up with her son. Her friends, Dwight and Rachel, had invited them to stay at their cabin on the edge of the BEN. A pair of Blue-Crowned Motmots called to each other. *Hoop-hoop* said one. *Hoop-hoop* said the other.

From the opposite side of the path, Peter saw it snap an insect out of the air. "Hoop-hoop!" called Peter, imitating the birds. Rachel heard them coming. "I see you've met the Motmots!" she said.

Blue-crowned Motmot
(*Momotus momota*)

The Blue-crowned Motmot has two things most other birds don't have. It has two long tail feathers that swing slowly back and forth like a pendulum. And its strong beak has edges like a saw blade perfect for catching and holding beetles, cicadas, spiders, butterflies, small lizards and even snakes. Often they whack their prey on a branch until it is quite dead before swallowing it. Motmots dig a long burrow in the ground with a nest at the end.

Strangler Fig
(*Ficus tuerckheimii*)

Did you ever see a tree that grows from the top down instead of up, whose roots dangle in the air? A monkey, a bat or a bird poops out the seed from fig fruits it has eaten while perched in a different tree. When the fig seed sprouts on a branch in the treetop, it sends down roots. Over decades the fig's aerial roots reach the ground and fuse, looking somewhat like pretzels. The fig doesn't actually "strangle" the host tree, but encloses and shades it until it eventually dies. As the host tree rots, it feeds the Strangler Fig creating buttress roots and helping it grow bigger and bigger until it finally becomes a hollow cylinder perfect for climbing up inside.

Brown Tent-making Bat
(*Uroderma magnirostrum*)

Why would a bat make a tent? And how? Bats need a protected place to roost during the day, but many rainforests don't have caves. What rainforests do have is lots of big leaves. Tent bats nibble along the mid vein of a large leaf, punching little holes until it is weakened enough to bend and droop, creating a tent-like roof under which they hang. They move to different leaves frequently and roost in small groups that help them stay warm. Half of Monteverde's 121 mammal species are bats. Unlike insect-eating bats in North America, many Costa Rican bats eat fruit. They are a big help in replanting the forest because they poop as they fly. The seeds get dropped in open areas and regrow the forest.

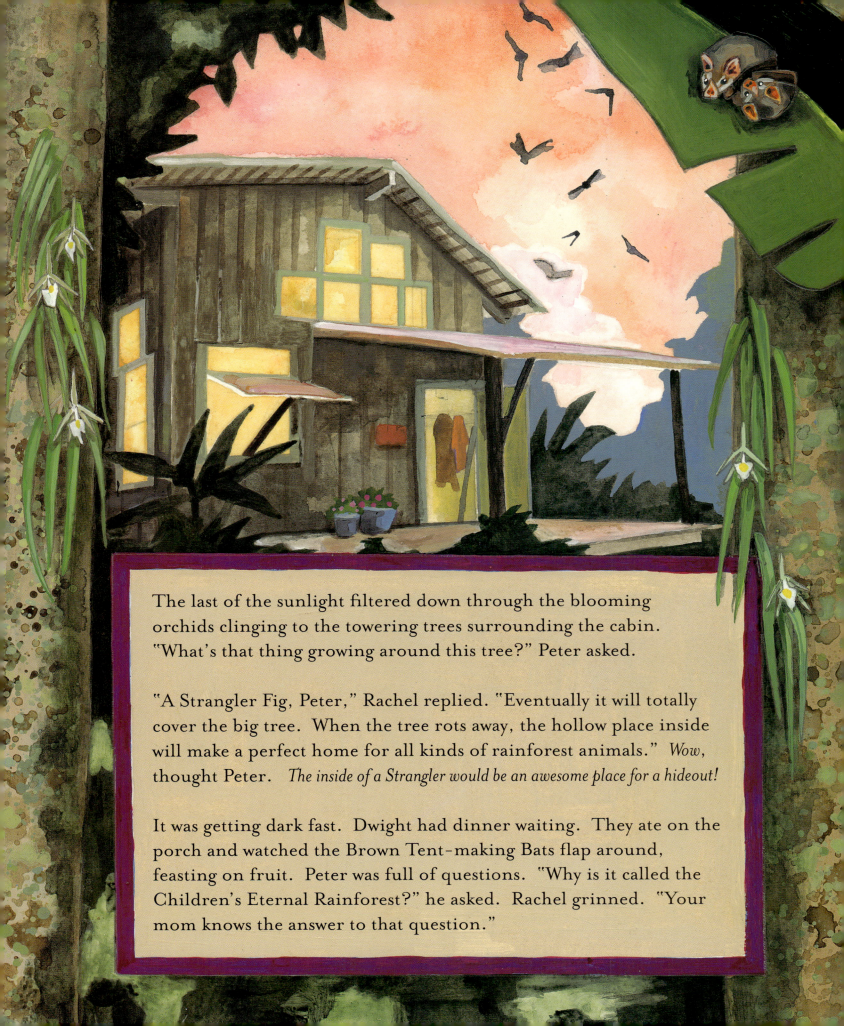

The last of the sunlight filtered down through the blooming orchids clinging to the towering trees surrounding the cabin. "What's that thing growing around this tree?" Peter asked.

"A Strangler Fig, Peter," Rachel replied. "Eventually it will totally cover the big tree. When the tree rots away, the hollow place inside will make a perfect home for all kinds of rainforest animals." *Wow,* thought Peter. *The inside of a Strangler would be an awesome place for a hideout!*

It was getting dark fast. Dwight had dinner waiting. They ate on the porch and watched the Brown Tent-making Bats flap around, feasting on fruit. Peter was full of questions. "Why is it called the Children's Eternal Rainforest?" he asked. Rachel grinned. "Your mom knows the answer to that question."

"A long time ago," said his mom, "a second grade class learned about the animals and plants that live in the rainforest. They wanted to protect this place forever for the kids of the future."

Rachel served fried bananas in chocolate sauce for dessert. Just like Peter, Kinkajous also love bananas, even very ripe ones. A mother Kinkajou and her baby sat on the roof, eating bananas that they had picked from a nearby tree. They curled their tails around their feet and blinked their big eyes in the dusk. The baby Kinkajou was a very messy eater. He got banana slop all over his face! But don't worry—he had a super-long tongue, so he just licked the rest of his dinner off his nose!

Kinkajou
(Potos flavus)

When you think of pollinators, you probably picture bees and wasps. Did you know that mammals can be pollinators, too? The Kinkajou with its very long, pointy tongue can reach deep within large blossoms for nectar. At the same time it gets pollen all over its nose. Heading for the next blossom, and the next, the Kinkajou spreads the pollen through the forest canopy. It loves juicy fruits and sometimes hangs upside down by its prehensile tail to catch the drips. But their favorite food is wild figs. Another cool feature the Kinkajou has is hind feet that can turn backwards! That way its claws can grip when it climbs down a tree headfirst. These members of the raccoon family communicate by barks, chittering, and shrill quavering calls. They also scent mark from glands in bare places on the sides of their faces, at the corner of their mouths, on their throats and tummies. They rub these glands on branches to communicate with other Kinkajous.

Paca
(Agouti paca)

The best thing about Pacas is that they are so delicious. The worst thing about Pacas is that there aren't very many left. Hunters love to eat Paca and also get top dollar for Paca meat in the market. Outside of protected areas Pacas are hard to find. They are nocturnal, well-camouflaged, and quiet as they forage for fruits, roots, stems, seeds and leaves in the night. Their huge eyes help them see in the dark. Pacas are the largest rodents in Central America. When male Pacas defend their territories, they try to bluff the other Paca by rumbling and teeth chittering. If that doesn't work, they stand head-to-head slashing at each other with their large incisors. Pacas like to be near streams so they can escape into the water in time of danger. Pacas are good swimmers. They even poop in the water on purpose so predators can't track and find them by scent as easily. Pretty smart!

"So how could a class of kids protect this whole big forest?" Peter asked.

"They did things that kids can do!" his mom replied. "They put on a puppet show, sold tickets, and gave the money to buy some rainforest."

Dwight cleared away some dishes and spread out a map on the table. "See, Peter? Here's what happens when kids work together. Look how big the BEN is now!" Peter was amazed. And sleepy.

As Peter put on his pajamas, he spotted a Paca poking around the porch. He slid into his sleeping bag, and listened to the rain pattering on the roof.

Peter thought he might sleep in a little bit. After all, he was on vacation. The Mantled Howler Monkeys didn't have the same idea. It was barely light when a troop of about 10 monkeys moved through the trees, singing their morning wakeup song as loud as they could. *"Whooooaaa Hooh Hooh Hoooh!"*

Peter jumped out of bed and opened the curtains to see what was going on. A baby Howler was hanging by his tail from a tree branch. *These guys are really silly,* thought Peter. SPLAT! A sloppy piece of fruit hit the window and slid down the glass. Peter laughed. He decided not to throw his breakfast back at the Howler Monkeys. He knew Rachel and Dwight planned a big hike for today.

Mantled Howler Monkey
(Alouatta palliata)

What makes the Howler Monkey the loudest land animal on the planet? A specialized bone made of soft cartilage vibrates inside the Howler's large throat chamber. Just like a cello makes a deeper sound than a smaller violin with its larger hollow resonator, so the Howler's enlarged throat chamber helps create an enormous roar heard for miles across the rainforest. Every morning the alpha male in each troop of Howlers bellows out his "dawn chorus" to let other troops know where his group is feeding for the day. The Howler uses its prehensile tail to grip and hold. Monkeys in the Old World (Africa and Asia) don't have prehensile tails. Using their strong tails as a fifth arm, Howlers can dangle and reach more of their favorite leaves and fruits.

Hoffman's Two-toed Sloth
(Choloepus hoffmanni)

Who has two toes on the front and three toes on the back? You would know if you had ever "hung out" with a sloth. A Two-toed Sloth is a very slo-o-o-ow mammal with really long arms. An entire ecosystem lives in its fur, especially algae, making it look like a green blob of moss. Sloth moths also live in the fur. Once a week, the sloth climbs to the ground to defecate, and the moths fly out of its fur and lay their eggs on the poop. When they mature, the new sloth moths will fly away to find another sloth. Sloths have a difficult time walking, but their shoulders are formed perfectly for hanging upside down.

Orchids
(this one is Oerstedella centradenia)

Many trees in the BEN are covered with hundreds of varieties of orchids that are "air plants" or epiphytes—plants that never touch the ground. Some orchid blossoms are so tiny you'll need a magnifying glass to see them. Some flower for only a day or two. Many grow only in the top of the canopy and can't be seen from the ground. Scientists keep discovering new orchids as they explore the canopy.

Anna and Dwight loaded backpacks into the jeep. As they drove to the trailhead, Peter noticed that a fine mist hung in the air. It wasn't raining, but water dripped from the tip of every leaf. *So that's why they call this a cloud forest*, Peter thought. *I've always wondered what it's like to be inside a cloud!*

As soon as they started hiking, Peter became so busy looking with his binoculars, that he walked straight into Anna's backpack! Then he saw something odd. "There's a pile of moss up in that tree," he said. "Hey! The moss has arms!"

"That's not a moss, Peter, it's a sloth!" Anna said.
"And it's covered with algae, not moss." added Rachel.
Wow...that's the best camouflage I've ever seen, thought Peter.

Resplendent Quetzal
(Pharomachrus mocinno)

Ancient Maya people believed there was a creature that was half bird and half snake, a feathered serpent. Try saying its name... Quetzalcoatl! (Ket-sal-co-AH-tel) Its glittering feathers change color in the sunlight. Its tail feathers are so long and graceful that ancient Maya kings wore them as a royal headdress. The males show off by flying high into the air above the forest and nosediving straight down into the trees. Quetzals are great spitters. Their favorite food, the tiny wild avocados, have large seeds that quetzals spit out—which is a great help in replanting the forest.

The Elfin Forest

High winds sweep across the mountaintop, so only gnarly dwarf-sized trees can survive here—tall trees would blow over. Blasting winds drive clouds through the elfin forest, leaving it dripping wet, the perfect home for mosses, bromeliads, ferns and orchids. Costa Rica is the "orchid capital of the world" with over 1500 different species, many of them epiphytes.

Soon they stood on the top of a narrow ridge. Damp clouds rolled over the hills, watering the lush forests that stretched out below them in both directions. They were standing on the continental divide —water on one side flowed to the Atlantic Ocean, while water on the other side flowed to the Pacific. A Resplendent Quetzal swooped overhead. Peter got a good look at the bird's bright red breast and trailing green tail feathers.

It was hard to believe that one second grade class could protect this whole rainforest.

"Mom, are the kids that started the BEN still in school?" he asked. "I don't think so," she replied. "One of them became your mom!"

"Mom, your class was really awesome," said Peter, as they hiked down to the San Gerardo Field Station, where they would spend the night.

"We had a great class, Peter, but it wasn't just us," she replied. "We told our friends, and they told their friends, and before long there were kids from several countries all working together."

"Children from 44 countries all over the world have sent donations to the BEN," said Dwight. "Their help has made it grow much bigger."

"Wow, that's so—" *BONK! squeak.* "What's that?" The noise was so loud that Peter covered his ears. *BONK! squeak.* "That's a Three-wattled Bellbird," shouted Rachel over the racket. "One of the loudest birds on the planet!" *If only the Bellbird could travel around the world,* Peter thought, *it would really spread word about the BEN.*

Three-wattled Bellbird
(Procnias tricarunculata)

Most birds attract females with their beautiful songs or their colorful feathers, but the Three-wattled Bellbird has unique strategies. His common name could be "Loudmouth" as his distinctive call can be heard a mile away. He usually perches on a bare branch high above the treetops and calls to attract females. If a younger male tries to take over the perch by landing on the outer part of the branch, the Three-wattled Bellbird will scoot his competitor closer and closer to the end of the branch and then open his beak and BONK right in the young Bellbird's ear until he falls off. May the loudest bird win! The Bellbird's other weird feature is his three long wormlike wattles that hang from the base of his beak.

Wild Avocado
(Ocotea tonduzii)

Wild avocados the size of olives are the favorite food of Bellbirds, Quetzals, Guans and many other species. There are over 70 kinds of wild avocado trees in the Monteverde forest.

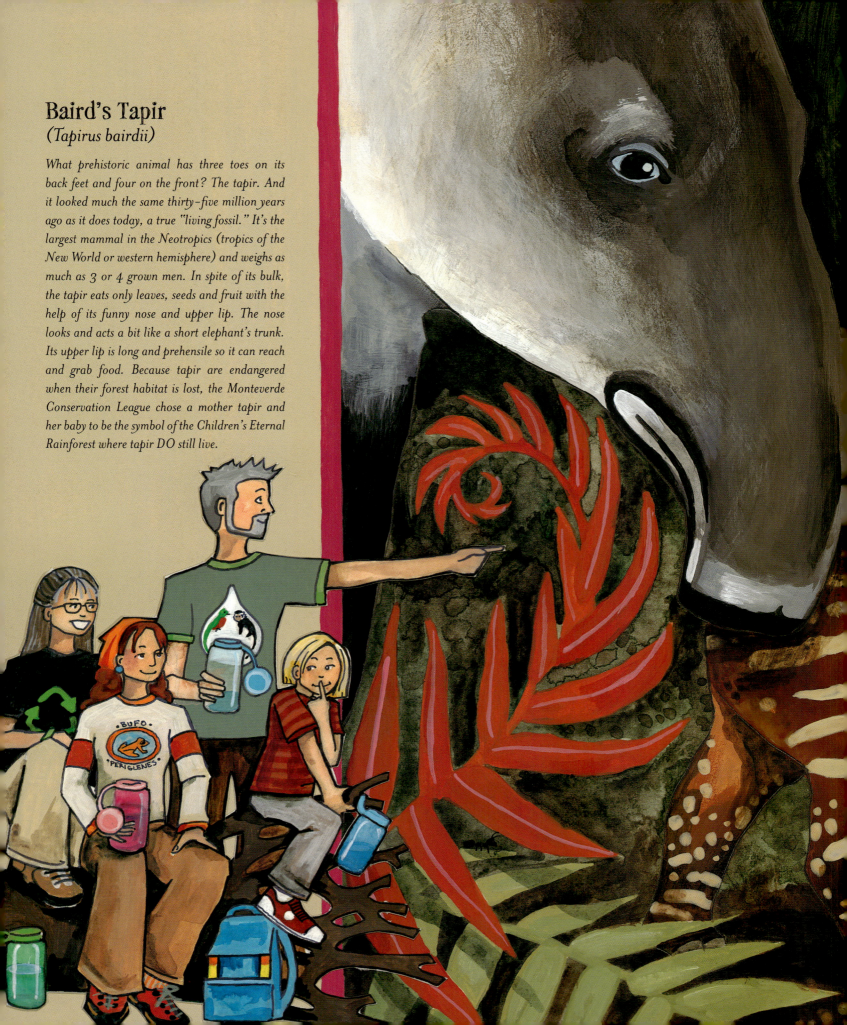

Baird's Tapir
(Tapirus bairdii)

What prehistoric animal has three toes on its back feet and four on the front? The tapir. And it looked much the same thirty-five million years ago as it does today, a true "living fossil." It's the largest mammal in the Neotropics (tropics of the New World or western hemisphere) and weighs as much as 3 or 4 grown men. In spite of its bulk, the tapir eats only leaves, seeds and fruit with the help of its funny nose and upper lip. The nose looks and acts a bit like a short elephant's trunk. Its upper lip is long and prehensile so it can reach and grab food. Because tapir are endangered when their forest habitat is lost, the Monteverde Conservation League chose a mother tapir and her baby to be the symbol of the Children's Eternal Rainforest where tapir DO still live.

A little while later, the hikers stopped for a water break. They sat quietly for a few minutes to rest and listen to the sounds of the forest. *I wonder how I could help the rainforest?* Peter thought.

Suddenly, Dwight pointed into the trees. Nobody said a word. A big mama Baird's Tapir lumbered through the underbrush, whistling softly to the tapir baby trotting by her side. Peter almost missed seeing the baby because it was covered with light spots and stripes, just like baby deer, so it blended with the dappled light of the rainforest.

Leaf-cutter Ants
(Atta cephalotes)

Did you know Leaf-cutter Ants are farmers? They cut and carry the leaves to their huge underground colonies. They chew the leaves up and use them as a fluffy "soil" in their garden. This special fungus is the ants' only food and is found nowhere else in the world. One queen ant has millions of workers in her colony. Much like T-shirts, the workers come in three sizes: small, medium and large. The large ants are soldiers that guard the colony and protect the trails. The medium-sized ants cut and carry the leaves and work underground. The little ones are tiny hitchhikers who ride on the cut leaves to protect the medium ones from wasps who lay their eggs on the heads of the medium-sized ants. When the wasp egg hatches, the larva will eat the head of the worker ant. So the hitchhiker's job is to get rid of the wasp egg and protect the ant. That's teamwork. They are also garbage collectors removing dead ant bodies to special underground trash chambers.

Peter was thinking it was lots easier to hike down the hill than up it, when he noticed a line of Leaf-cutter Ants marching back and forth across the trail. "Don't step on the Leaf-cutter Ants, anyone!" Peter announced. The hikers crouched down to watch the ants haul leaf pieces back to their nests. Right next to the ant trail, he saw several huge paw prints in the mud.

"Hey, check this out!" called Peter. "Who made these tracks?"

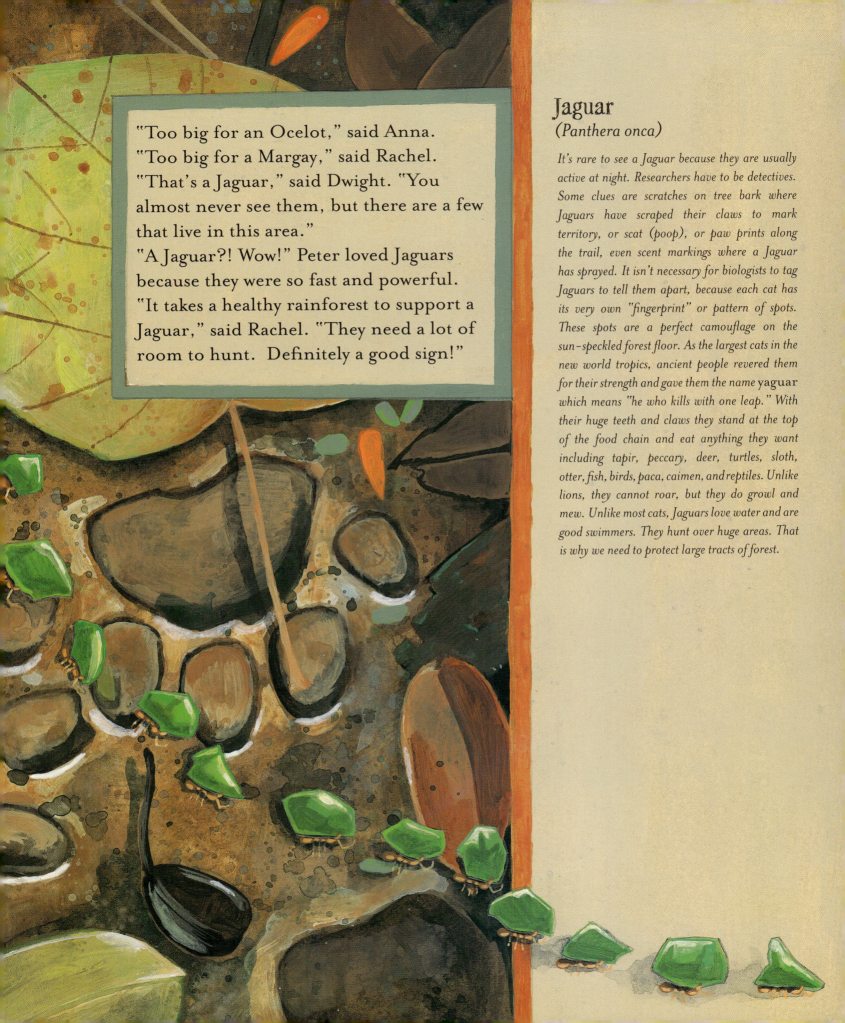

"Too big for an Ocelot," said Anna.
"Too big for a Margay," said Rachel.
"That's a Jaguar," said Dwight. "You almost never see them, but there are a few that live in this area."
"A Jaguar?! Wow!" Peter loved Jaguars because they were so fast and powerful.
"It takes a healthy rainforest to support a Jaguar," said Rachel. "They need a lot of room to hunt. Definitely a good sign!"

Jaguar
(Panthera onca)

It's rare to see a Jaguar because they are usually active at night. Researchers have to be detectives. Some clues are scratches on tree bark where Jaguars have scraped their claws to mark territory, or scat (poop), or paw prints along the trail, even scent markings where a Jaguar has sprayed. It isn't necessary for biologists to tag Jaguars to tell them apart, because each cat has its very own "fingerprint" or pattern of spots. These spots are a perfect camouflage on the sun-speckled forest floor. As the largest cats in the new world tropics, ancient people revered them for their strength and gave them the name yaguar *which means "he who kills with one leap." With their huge teeth and claws they stand at the top of the food chain and eat anything they want including tapir, peccary, deer, turtles, sloth, otter, fish, birds, paca, caimen, and reptiles. Unlike lions, they cannot roar, but they do growl and mew. Unlike most cats, Jaguars love water and are good swimmers. They hunt over huge areas. That is why we need to protect large tracts of forest.*

Rufous-eyed Stream Frog
(Duellmanohyla rufioculis)

The Rufous-eyed Stream Frog could be called the "Mystery Frog." No one knows exactly what it eats or where the female goes in the daytime. She's difficult to see because she is small, closes her big rusty-reddish eyes, and flattens her body against a leaf the same color she is. Perfect camouflage!

What we do know is they have sticky round pads on the tips of their toes to grip on slippery leaves. The male calls from his leafy perch just above the stream to attract females. His call sounds like two pebbles knocking together. Toxic chemicals in their skin protect them from predators.

Endemic to Costa Rica, they live in a few areas at the head of streams deep in the forest. "Endemic" means lives in only one place in the world. The Childrens' Eternal Rainforest is one of the most important protected refuges for them.

The hikers arrived at the San Gerardo Field Station just in time for dinner. Then Mark, a British naturalist, took them on a night hike. At first, Peter couldn't stop talking about all the animals and plants he had seen during the daytime. But he didn't want to miss all the night animals, so he started listening instead. After walking for a while, they stood still and turned off their flashlights. Peter tried to count the sounds. *Dripping water, insects, bats, frogs, my own breathing…*

Mark explained what they were hearing. "That's a Dink Frog…there's the Spot-Shouldered Rain Frog, and right here…" Mark flipped on his flashlight in the direction of the headwater of a tiny stream "…are two Rufous-eyed Stream Frogs. You're not likely to find them outside of Monteverde. The Rufous-Eyed Stream Frog might not have survived without the BEN."

Peter spent the rest of the night thinking about how to help the BEN.

He thought about the Blue Morphos and the Blue-crowned Motmots.
He thought about the Strangler Figs and the Brown Tent-making Bats.
He thought about the wide-eyed Kinkajous and the sneaky Pacas.
He thought about the noisy Howler Monkeys in the morning.
He thought about the Two-toed Sloths, and Three-wattled Bellbirds.
He thought about the baby Baird's Tapir and the Resplendent Quetzal.
He thought about the speedy Leaf-cutter Ants, the stealthy Jaguar…
          and the teeny-tiny Rufous-eyed Stream Frog…

Reforestation

Although the BEN protects over 50,000 acres, it is only an "island" of rainforest. Beyond its borders, vast areas have been cut to raise crops and cattle, leaving a patchwork of isolated forests remaining. Many animals will not or cannot move through open fields—they need the forest for food and protection. The BEN and its associated organizations are working to connect these islands of forest by planting corridors that link the remaining forest. Tree roots also hold the soil in place and help streams to keep flowing. When native trees, like wild avocadoes, are replanted, migrating birds, like quetzals, can safely get to the food sources they need when the seasons change. Hundreds of thousands of baby trees have been given to farmers to plant as windbreaks and corridors. Hundreds of volunteers have helped replant, too.

...then he knew just how he could help!

How the Children's Eternal Rainforest Came to Be...

THIS IS THE 1987 FIRST AND SECOND GRADE CLASS IN FAGERVIK, SWEDEN, WITH THEIR TEACHER EHA KERN, THAT HAD THE IDEA TO SAVE A TROPICAL RAINFOREST BY RAISING MONEY TO BUY THE LAND.

RACHEL CRANDELL PEERS OUT FROM AN OPENING IN A HOLLOW STRANGLER FIG TREE.

DWIGHT AND RACHEL CRANDELL'S CABIN IN MONTEVERDE, COSTA RICA.

In 1951, a group of American Quakers who were looking for a peace-loving country to live in, immigrated to Costa Rica. They purchased 3,000 acres of mountainous rainforest and set aside 1,400 of those acres as Costa Rica's first rainforest preserve. They named it El Bosque Eterno, The Eternal Forest. They named their community Monteverde, or "Green Mountain."

In 1972, biologist George Powell went to Monteverde to study the resplendent quetzal. He deemed this cloud forest so special that he encouraged conservation organizations to protect more land in the area. Especially with the help of Wolf Guindon, one of the Quakers, the Monteverde Cloud Forest Preserve was created.

In 1987, the first and second grade students in Eha Kern's class in Fagervik, Sweden were learning about tropical rainforests. They were fascinated by the amazing array of wildlife, but were concerned when they learned that many of the rainforests were being cut and burned to make way for farms. An American botanist, Professor Sharon Kinsman of Bates College in Lewiston, Maine, was visiting Sweden. She knew the Monteverde Cloud Forest Preserve and was excited about the biodiversity she found there. Eha invited Sharon to tell the class about it.

When that class in Fagervik, Sweden learned about the rainforest, they wanted to do something to help. They decided to raise money. They put on a play and sold tickets. They organized a bunny-hopping contest. They gave pony rides. They sold home-baked goodies. Their goal was to raise enough money to buy and save 25 acres, but their enthusiasm grew and so did their fundraising ideas. A newspaper article was written about their efforts, then a television report was aired. Other kids heard about it, and more schools began to raise funds too. The Swedish government matched funds raised by the children. In the first year they raised over $100,000. That is how the Children's Rainforest (Barnens Regnskog in Swedish) was born.

Sharon helped arrange for threatened forest to be added to the BEN. She also founded "Children's Rainforest USA" to help kids in the United States participate in the campaign. The idea swept the world. Eventually, children in 44 countries contributed. Bernd Kern, Eha's husband, helped the international efforts by keeping people in touch and helping to set up sister organizations in Sweden, Germany, United Kingdom, Canada and Japan. By 1995, El Bosque Eterno de los Niños ("Children's Eternal Rainforest" in Spanish) commonly called the BEN, protected 54,000 acres and had become the largest private reserve in Central America.

Unfortunately, it was necessary to hire guards to protect the forest. Otherwise, poachers would illegally hunt animals for meat and for their pelts, or steal endangered orchids to sell to collectors, or catch colorful frogs and birds to sell as pets, or cut and sell endangered trees. Sometimes they even tried to clear land and plant crops inside the BEN!

In addition, rainforest corridors need to be created so that as the dry and wet seasons change, animals can migrate down from the mountaintops in the BEN to find food in the few remaining patches of undisturbed rainforest at lower altitudes. To help, the Monteverde Conservation League U.S. (MCLUS) was founded in 2002 to help raise money for additional land purchase, more guards, and environmental education. Also a group of enthusiastic students in Vermont began to raise money for critical habitat—they call themselves the "Change the World Kids." By 2007, the 20th anniversary of the BEN, the MCLUS had raised over a quarter of a million dollars. Children around the world are beginning to write the next chapter of this story.

Edmund Burke once said, "Nobody makes a greater mistake than he who does nothing because he could only do a little." Thanks go to the little Swedish kids long ago who chose to do something. They began to protect tropical rainforest and many friends have helped since. Now the Children's Eternal Forest has a chance to be a forest ... forever.

May the forest be with you,
                Rachel & Kristin

Special thanks to the friends and biologists who helped us make this book as accurate as possible:
Judy Arroyo, Federico Chinchilla, Dwight Crandell, Deb DeRosier, Frank Joyce, Eha Kern, Sharon Kinsman, Richard Laval, Carlos Muñoz, Giselle Rodriguez, Mark Wainwright, Jim Wolfe, Willow Zuchowski.

KRISTIN PAINTING THE TITLE PAGE FOR 'THE FOREVER FOREST' - RIGHT IN THE BEN!

HUNDREDS OF BABY TREES READY TO BE PLANTED IN PLACES WHERE THE RAINFOREST WAS CHOPPED DOWN

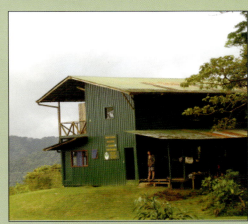

SAN GERARDO FIELD STATION

How To Learn More About Tropical Rainforests:

Books:

Children Saved the Rain Forest by Dorothy Patent (1996):
> Packed with information about the cloud forest, this book celebrates the Swedish children who started the BEN.

A Walk in the Rainforest by Kristin Joy Pratt (1992):
> This is an alphabet book written on two levels—for young children as well as for older children or adults, which follows XYZ the Ant on his walk through the forest.

The Great Kapok Tree by Lynne Cherry (1990):
> This lushly illustrated book introduces the reader to the animal families of a Brazilian rainforest, with a plea for protection.

Flute's Journey by Lynne Cherry (1997):
> A neo-tropical migrating wood thrush makes a perilous journey from the Children's Eternal Rainforest in Costa Rica to Maryland.

When the Monkeys Came Back by Kristine Franklin (1994):
> This book traces the life of Doña Marta and how she replants the forest and restores the wildlife.

The Lorax by Dr. Seuss (1971, 2004):
> Here is the classic story of foolish waste of a forest and loss of biodiversity with a ray of hope at the end.

The Cloud Forest by Sneed Collard (2001):
> This is a beautifully illustrated close-up look at the plants and animals that inhabit the Monteverde cloud forest.

It's Our World Too by Phillip Hoose (1993):
> This collection of true stories about children who have helped the world be a better place includes a story about the BEN which begins on page 83.

Websites:

Monteverde Conservation League US, Inc.
> www.mclus.org

Monteverde Conservation League
> www.acmcr.org

Monteverde Cloud Forest Preserve
> www.cloudforestalive.org

Costa Rican Conservation Foundation
> www.fccmonteverde.org

Change the World Kids
> www.changetheworldkids.com

Children's Rainforest of Sweden
> www.barnens-regnskog.net

Children's Rainforest U.K.
> www.tropical-forests.com

Children's Rainforest Japan
> www.jungle.rg.jp

Children's Rainforest Germany
> www.kinderregenwald.de

Roots and Shoots, Jane Goodall's program for youth
> www.rootsandshoots.org

Rainforest Action Network,
> www.ran.org/what_we_do/rainforessts_in_the_classroom

Rainforest Alliance
> www.rainforest-alliance.org/programs/education/

Missouri Botanical Garden
> www.mbgnet.net

To Find the BEN on Google Earth,

fly to 10 22' N, 84 43' W and click on search. Look for the big dark green patch of forested mountains south of Arenal Volcano and the big lake. Click on the nearby blue dots for photos of scenes near the BEN.

March 2007: Kristin Joy Pratt-Serafini and Rachel Crandell hike through the BEN down to the San Gerardo Field Station, just like Peter does in the story.

Kristin Joy Pratt-Serafini
www.xyzant.com

Kristin Joy Pratt-Serafini first connected her love of art with her concern for the rainforest when she wrote and illustrated A Walk in the Rainforest *as a freshman in high school. Since then, she has written and illustrated several other environmentally-focused books for children. She hopes her colorful paintings will get kids excited about going outside and exploring for themselves. Kristin first visited the BEN in 1997 as a college student, and was excited to go back with Rachel 10 years later, in March of 2007. As she wrote the story about Anna and Peter, and painted the animals and plants they saw, she could picture every step of their adventure through the rainforest… because she had just been to the BEN herself! Rachel took her on the same hike described in the story. She even saw the Rufous-eyed Stream Frogs on the night hike with Mark!*

Rachel Crandell
www.rainforestrachel.com

Rachel Crandell taught at Principia Lower School for 20 years after running a nursery school on their farm in Indiana. She and her husband started the Monteverde Conservation League, U.S. to help protect the Children's Eternal Rainforest. They have a cabin in Monteverde where they spend several months each year. Just like Peter and Anna in the story, her children and grandchildren have walked the paths, climbed the strangler fig, and heard the bellbird BONK. Besides researching and writing the scientific paragraphs for The Forever Forest, *Rachel has motivated thousands of children and adults to help protect the BEN. She is known as "Rainforest Rachel" because of the hundreds of presentations she has done for school groups about tropical rainforests, and the trips she leads to Costa Rica.*

Copyright © 2008
Kristin Joy Pratt-Serafini and Rachel Crandell
Illustrations copyright © 2008 Kristin Joy Pratt-Serafini

All rights reserved. No part of this book may be reproduced or transmitted to any form or by any means, electronic or mechanical, including photocopying, recording, or by any information and retrieval system, without written permission from the publisher.

Computer production by Patty Arnold, *Menagerie Design and Publishing*.

Dawn Publications
12402 Bitney Springs Road, Nevada City, CA 95959
530-274-7775 • nature@dawnpub.com

Manufactured by Regent Publishing Services, Hong Kong
Printed July 2019 in Shenzhen, Guangdong, China
10 9 8 7 6 5
First Edition

Library of Congress Cataloging-in-Publication Data
Pratt-Serafini, Kristin Joy.
 The forever forest : kids save a tropical treasure / Kristin Joy Pratt-Serafini, with Rachel Crandell ; illustrated by Kristin Joy Pratt-Serafini.
   p. cm.
 Summary: "On a hike through the Children's Eternal Rainforest, Peter discovers many intriguing plants and animals, and also that his mother was one of the second-graders who joined with other children from all over the world to make preservation of this Costa Rican rainforest possible"--Provided by publisher.
 Includes bibliographical references and index.
 ISBN-13: 978-1-58469-101-3 (hardback : alk. paper)
 ISBN-13: 978-1-58469-102-0 (pbk. : alk. paper)
 1. Bosque Eterno de los Niños (Costa Rica)--Juvenile literature. 2. Rain forest ecology--Costa Rica--Bosque Eterno de los Niños. I. Crandell, Rachel. II. Title.
 QH108.C6P73 2008
 578.734097286--dc22
                                    2007035606

ALSO BY KRISTIN JOY PRATT-SERAFINI

A Walk in the Rainforest — colorful, fresh and now a classic, this was illustrated with magic markers when Kristin was 15 years old.

A Swim through the Sea — using the same alliterative, alphabetical approach as her rainforest book, this was illustrated with watercolors when Kristin was 17 years old.

SOME OTHER NATURE AWARENESS BOOKS FROM DAWN PUBLICATIONS

How We Know What We Know about Our Changing Climate by Lynne Cherry and Gary Braasch — clearly presents evidence of climate change including patterns from birds, flowers, tree rings, mud cores, and much more, and how evidence is often gathered by young "citizen-scientists."

Over in the Jungle: A Rainforest Rhyme by Marianne Berkes, illustrated by Jeanette Canyon — this counting book captures a rain forest teeming with remarkable creatures.

Over in the Ocean: In a Coral Reef by Marianne Berkes, illustrated by Jeanette Canyon — with unique and outstanding style, this book portrays the vivid community of creatures that inhabit the ocean's coral reefs.

Over in the Forest: Come and Take a Peek by Marianne Berkes, illustrated by Jill Dubin — Children learn the ways of common forest animals and count their babies, all to the rhythm of the traditional tune "Over in the Meadow."

Wonderful Nature, Wonderful You by Karin Ireland, illustrated by Christopher Canyon — Nature can be a great teacher. With a light touch especially suited to children, this 20th Anniversary edition evokes feelings of calm acceptance, joy, and wonder.

A Moon of My Own by Jennifer Rustgi, illustrated by Ashley White — An adventurous young girl journeys around the world, if only in her dreams. She discovers natural beauty and manmade wonders, accompanied by her companion—the moon.

There's a Bug on My Book written and illustrated by John Himmelman — Children's imaginations will be engaged as they're introduced to all sorts of critters that hop, fly, wiggle, and slide across the pages of this book.

The Mouse and the Meadow written and illustrated by Chad Wallace — Experience the vibrant and sometimes dangerous nature of meadow life from a mouse's eye-view. Science blends seamlessly into the story.

Dawn Publications is dedicated to inspiring in children a deeper understanding and appreciation for all life on Earth. To view our titles or to order, please visit us at www.dawnpub.com, or call 800-545-7475.